Dear Parent:
Your child's love of reading starts here!

Every child learns to read in a different way and at his or her own speed. Some go back and forth between reading levels and read favorite books again and again. Others read through each level in order. You can help your young reader improve and become more confident by encouraging his or her own interests and abilities. From books your child reads with you to the first books he or she reads alone, there are I Can Read Books for every stage of reading:

SHARED READING
Basic language, word repetition, and whimsical illustrations, ideal for sharing with your emergent reader

BEGINNING READING
Short sentences, familiar words, and simple concepts for children eager to read on their own

READING WITH HELP
Engaging stories, longer sentences, and language play for developing readers

READING ALONE
Complex plots, challenging vocabulary, and high-interest topics for the independent reader

ADVANCED READING
Short paragraphs, chapters, and exciting themes for the perfect bridge to chapter books

I Can Read Books have introduced children to the joy of reading since 1957. Featuring award-winning authors and illustrators and a fabulous cast of beloved characters, I Can Read Books set the standard for beginning readers.

A lifetime of discovery begins with the magical words "I Can Read!"

Visit www.icanread.com for information
on enriching your child's reading experience.

Pete the Cat Goes Camping
Copyright © 2018 by James Dean
Pete the Cat is a registered trademark of Pete the Cat, LLC.
All rights reserved. Printed in China.
No part of this book may be used or reproduced in any manner whatsoever without written permission except
in the case of brief quotations embodied in critical articles and reviews. For information address HarperCollins
Children's Books, a division of HarperCollins Publishers, 195 Broadway, New York, NY 10007.
www.icanread.com

Library of Congress Control Number: 2018930211
ISBN 978-0-06-267530-9 (trade bdg.) —ISBN 978-0-06-267529-3 (pbk.)

Typography by Jeanne Hogle

21 22 SCP 21   ❖   First Edition

Pete the Cat

GOES CAMPING

by James Dean

HARPER

An Imprint of HarperCollinsPublishers

Pete is excited to go camping!
This is his first time.

"Don't forget your sleeping bag!"
says Dad.
"Or your hiking boots!" Mom says.

The campsite is deep in the woods.

Mom and Dad set up the tent.

Pete and Bob help collect sticks
so they can make a fire later.

Pete and Bob go for a hike.
Bob shows Pete the footprints
of different animals.

"Do you think
we will see anything cool?"
asks Pete.
"Maybe," says Bob.

Pete and his dad go fishing.

They must be very quiet

and very still to catch a fish.

Fishing takes a long time.

They finally catch some fish.

Mom builds a fire.

She cooks the fish for dinner.

It tastes yummy.

Next Pete toasts marshmallows.
Pete makes s'mores with
chocolate and graham crackers.

It starts to get dark out.
Bob tells Pete a story
about a scary, hairy giant.

The giant lives in the woods.

His name is Bigfoot.

"Do you think Bigfoot lives *here*?"
asks Pete.

"No one has ever seen Bigfoot,"
says Bob.

"Don't let Bob scare you," says Dad.

"Bigfoot is not real," Mom says.

Pete sighs with relief!

"But if he is real, I bet he's friendly," says Dad, "and likes s'mores too!"

That's not scary, thinks Pete.

Maybe he wants a s'more.

Pete leaves one for his hairy friend.

Soon it's time for bed.

"Lights out, boys!" Dad says.

Bob and Pete share a tent.

Pete gets into his sleeping bag.

It is cozy, but he cannot sleep.

The woods seem extra dark.

And all the sounds

seem extra loud at night.

Pete hears a weird swooshing sound.

"What is that?" he asks Bob.

"That's just the wind," says Bob.

Pete hears an odd chirping noise.

"What is that?" he asks out loud.

Those are just the crickets.

Pete hears a strange hooting sound.

"What is that?" he wonders.

That's just an owl.

Pete thinks of his friend Owl.

Pete hears a loud snapping sound.

CRACK!

"What is that?" he wonders.

But Bob is already fast asleep.

Pete listens carefully.

CRACK!

Is it Bigfoot?

Pete peeks outside.

It is too dark to see anything.

When Pete wakes up, he checks
the spot where he left
the s'more for Bigfoot.

The s'more is gone!

THANKS
FOR THE
TREAT
XOXO

There is a note.

It says, "Thanks for

the treat! XOXO"

Pete shows his family.

"Wow, I knew Bigfoot was real!"

says Bob.

31

Pete knows Bigfoot is not scary.
Just because he looks different
does not mean he is scary.
He even likes s'mores too!